Puf

THE SMELL

Rosemary Hayes runs a
Cambridgeshire, where s.
three children and an assortment of unruly animals.

Rosemary Hayes

The Smell That Got Away

Illustrated by Tony Blundell

PUFFIN BOOKS

For Class 4 (1991–92) at
Duxford Community School

PUFFIN BOOKS

Published by the Penguin Group
Penguin Books Ltd, 27 Wrights Lane, London W8 5TZ, England
Penguin Books USA Inc., 375 Hudson Street, New York, New York 10014, USA
Penguin Books Australia Ltd, Ringwood, Victoria, Australia
Penguin Books Canada Ltd, 10 Alcorn Avenue, Toronto, Ontario, Canada M4V 3B2
Penguin Books (NZ) Ltd, 182–190 Wairau Road, Auckland 10, New Zealand

Penguin Books Ltd, Registered Offices: Harmondsworth, Middlesex, England

First published by Viking 1992
Published in Puffin Books 1994
10 9 8 7 6 5 4 3 2 1

Text copyright © Rosemary Hayes, 1992
Illustrations copyright © Tony Blundell, 1992
All rights reserved

The moral right of the author has been asserted

Printed and bound in England by Clays Ltd, St Ives plc
Filmset in Times

Chapter One

It was Monday the fifth of September. The first day of term. Tom stood at the staff-room door and looked inside.

He stared for a moment, and then stared some more. His eyes got rounder and rounder and his mouth fell open. Then he turned and ran all the way to his classroom.

"I've seen him! I've seen him!" he panted, as he burst into the room and dropped his school-bag on the floor.

"Who?" asked Matthew.

"Him – the new teacher. He's arrived!"

The rest of Class 4 stopped talking and gathered round Tom.

"How old is he?"

"I dunno. About a hundred."

"What's he look like?"

"He's *wild*!"

Just then, the door was flung open and the new teacher strode into the classroom.

Mr Bentwhistle had arrived.

He was extremely tall and thin, with a big beaky nose, frizzy hair and dark bushy eyebrows. He moved his eyebrows up and down very fast, sometimes together and sometimes not.

On his huge feet were long red boots, and tucked into these was a pair of faded jeans. He wore a glittering shirt and over his shoulders hung a bright yellow cloak.

Mr Bentwhistle had a pile of books under one arm, and under the other a large pink box. He slapped the books down on the table and placed the box, very gently, beside them.

Then he looked at Class 4. And Class 4 looked back at him.

Mr Bentwhistle undid his cloak and whirled it round his head a few times. Every pair of eyes in Class 4 followed it round and round, and watched it drift gently in the air and down on to the back of the chair.

Mr Bentwhistle pointed a long finger at Matthew.

"You! What's your name?"

"Matthew," stuttered Matthew.

Mr Bentwhistle then pointed at the pile of books. "Hand these round, Matthew."

While Matthew handed round the books, Mr Bentwhistle went over to the window and stared at the yard outside.

When Tom got his book, he whispered to Matthew, "He's nuts!"

Mr Bentwhistle didn't turn round. He carried on staring

out of the window.

"Boy at the back there," he said suddenly. "Boy with the fair hair and Batman T-shirt."

Tom jumped. It was him!

"I am not nuts, and you would do well to remember it! I am very far from nuts. I see everything, I hear everything, and I know everything."

Tom stared at Matthew, but they didn't dare say anything.

He must have eyes in the back of his head, thought Tom.

"No," said Mr Bentwhistle. "I do not have eyes in the back of my head."

Tom's mouth went dry. Mr

Bentwhistle could read his thoughts!

"But," went on Mr Bentwhistle, "I do have something to help me. Something rather special."

He turned from the window and went back to the table. Then he stroked the pink box very gently.

"What's in the box?" someone asked.

"Hush," thundered Mr Bentwhistle. "No more questions!"

He gave the box one last stroke. Then, bringing together his dancing eyebrows in a fierce frown, he faced the class.

"Open your books," he said.

Chapter Two

At the end of school, Mr
Bentwhistle picked up his
books and his pink box, rubbed
the side of his nose with his

finger, and walked towards the door. The class watched, amazed, as his yellow cloak suddenly rose up by itself. For a moment it hung in the air, and then it followed Mr Bentwhistle.

Matthew turned to Tom, "He's weird."

"I wonder if he's got a family," said Tom.

"Shouldn't think so," said Matthew.

"Do you think he lives in an ordinary house, like ours?"

Matthew shook his head. "I can't see him in an ordinary house, can you?"

Suddenly Tom had an idea. He looked round to make sure that no one was listening. Then he whispered, "Let's follow him."

They picked up their school-bags and ran out into the yard.

"Look!" said Tom, taking hold of Matthew's arm. "Over there!"

"Where?"

"There. Behind the hedge. Can't you see?"

Mr Bentwhistle's yellow cloak and dark frizzy hair could just be seen, bobbing quickly up and down. The boys had to run to keep him in sight as he turned down a side street. They climbed up a hill which got steeper and steeper, but Mr Bentwhistle didn't slow down. In fact, he seemed to be going faster.

"I've got a pain in my side," panted Matthew.

Tom was red in the face and his school-bag was getting heavier and heavier. He was too puffed to answer.

Just when they felt they couldn't go another step, they reached the top of the hill. They stopped to rest for a moment, while Mr Bentwhistle strode off ahead.

"I've never been here before," said Matthew, looking round him. "We must be right above the town."

He turned and looked behind him. Then he said, "That's funny."

20

"What?" said Tom.

"I can't see the town any more. It all looks different," said Matthew.

Tom turned to look too. Then he shrugged: "I expect we've come further than we thought." He shifted his bag on to the other shoulder. "Come on, we're going to lose him if we don't hurry."

They started to run after Mr Bentwhistle. They were out in the country now, with fields and trees all round them.

"He can't live here," said Tom. "There aren't any houses."

But just as he spoke, Mr Bentwhistle stopped, climbed over a fence and went into a field. He put down his box and

his books carefully and gave a
huge stretch.

"What's he doing? There's
nothing there!" said Matthew.

"Yes there is!"

Tom was right. All by itself
in the middle of the field stood
a tall yellow house.

"But it wasn't there just now!" gasped Matthew.

"Shh," said Tom. "Watch!"

They watched as Mr Bentwhistle put his fingers in his mouth and whistled. He gave one long whistle, then two short whistles.

"Look!" said Tom, and then "Wow!", as the front door of the house swung open.

Mr Bentwhistle ran up the stairs to the front door and went inside. The door closed behind him.

"What now?" said Matthew.

"I dunno," said Tom. "Let's wait and see what happens."

They didn't have long to wait. A few moments later, the door opened again, and Mr Bentwhistle came out with a large black animal by his side.

"He's going to take the dog

for a walk," said Tom, but his voice was unsure. The animal didn't *look* much like a dog.

"Don't be a wally," said Matthew. "That's not a dog!"

"What is it then?" asked Tom, as they watched it bound off, with the sun shining on its sleek black fur.

"That's a panther," said Matthew.

"A *panther*!" Tom gulped.

But soon Mr Bentwhistle and the panther were far away, heading for the distant woods.

"Let's go home now," said Tom. "We know where he lives."

"No," said Matthew firmly. "Not before we've seen the house."

"But the door's closed," said Tom. "We can't get inside."

"It might not be locked," said Matthew.

So they crept up to the door and tried the handle.

"It is locked," said Tom, and ran back down the steps. "Come on, let's go."

"No, wait," said Matthew. He put down his school-bag and put his fingers in his mouth.

He gave one long whistle, then two short whistles.

They heard a faint click and
watched as the door handle
turned, all by itself, and the
door opened. It was only a
crack, but it *was* open.

"You go first," said Tom. He felt quite scared.

"No," said Matthew, "*you* go first." He pushed Tom forward.

Tom climbed up the steps. At the top, he turned and looked down at Matthew.

"Go on!" said Matthew.

Tom faced the door. Then, very slowly, he edged inside, ready to run back down the steps at any moment.

His heart was thumping and his hands were sweaty. He kept his eyes tight shut until he was inside.

He waited, but nothing

happened. At last, he opened
his eyes – and his mouth
dropped open in surprise.

In front of him was an
enormous room, and stacked
from floor to ceiling were
hundreds and hundreds of
boxes, all brightly coloured
and all different sizes.

"Matthew," he called.
"Come and look."

Slowly, Matthew followed
him into the room.

31

"Hey, this is wild! There's no
furniture or anything. Why's
he got all these boxes?" said
Matthew.

"Let's get one and see what's

inside," said Tom.

He took a dark blue box from the top of the nearest pile.

Matthew peered out of the door. "Quick," he said. "Mr Bentwhistle's coming back."

Tom put the box under his arm and they ran out of the room, down the steps and back the way they'd come.

Chapter Three

They ran until the yellow house was far behind them. Then they stopped and sat down by some trees.

"Open up," said Matthew.

Tom shook the blue box.

"*Open* it!" said Matthew again. "Hurry up!"

Tom slowly lifted up the lid and looked inside.

The next moment, he had thrown it to the ground.

"There's nothing in it!" he said. "It's empty!"

"Here, I'll take a look," said Matthew. He took the lid right off, turned the box upside down and banged on the bottom.

A tiny scrap of paper floated to the ground. Matthew picked it up.

"Higglefizz," he read.

"Higglefizz!" repeated Tom. "What does that mean?"

"I haven't a clue," said Matthew, with a shrug. Then he jumped up, crumpled the scrap of paper and kicked the box into the bushes. "Come on," he said, dragging Tom to his feet. "It's nothing but a big con. We'd better get home."

They started to walk back the way they had come. Or, at least, they *thought* it was the way they'd come. But nothing looked the same. And as they were walking, they breathed in a strange, sweet smell.

Wherever they went, it
followed them.

Tom said, "What shall we
do? We're never going to find
the way home."

Suddenly, there was a rustle
behind them. They both
jumped and spun round.

Mr Bentwhistle stood there, his arms folded, his cloak floating in the wind, and his black frizzy hair in a wild tangle. He looked down at the two boys from his great height, and his bushy eyebrows went up, then down, then sideways.

"Lost?" he asked, in a terribly loud voice.

They nodded and looked down at the ground.

Mr Bentwhistle said nothing, and for a few moments there was an awkward silence. Then he began to sniff. First he pressed one side of his nose and sniffed with one nostril.

Then he pressed the other side of his nose and sniffed with the other nostril. Then he looked hard at Tom and Matthew.

They felt his stare pierce right down to their toes.

"Hmm," he muttered, "I *think* I smell Higglefizz." He sniffed again, with both nostrils. "Yes, I'm sure it's Higglefizz."

The boys said nothing, and carried on staring at the ground.

"Well, well, well. Higglefizz, eh!" said Mr Bentwhistle.

Then he started to laugh. His whole body rocked from side to side, his cloak rippled over his shoulders, and his eyebrows shot about his face.

At last, he stopped laughing and wiped his eyes. Then he stretched out his hand and pointed.

"Follow my finger," he bellowed, "and you'll be home before you know it."

Matthew and Tom looked to where he was pointing. And there was the road, as clear as anything!

Chapter Four

The next morning, Tom and Matthew felt rather strange.

They smelt strange too.

And when they spoke, some *very* strange words came out.

They started to walk to
school.

"Piddlescotch," said Tom.

"Numbum," said Matthew.

As they turned a corner,
Matthew suddenly grabbed
Tom's arm and pointed,
"Hobblegobs!" he said.

"Loopy hobblegobs!"
repeated Tom.

Some dogs were running
down the road towards them,
and they were running very
fast. Not just one or two dogs,
but twenty, thirty, or even
forty dogs. There were big
dogs, small dogs, smart dogs
and scruffy dogs.

There was a crowd of people following the dogs. They were waving their arms and calling out, "Fido", "Lassie", "Benjie", "Popsy", "Hector", "Pepper".

Tom and Matthew turned round and started to run away. But even more dogs came towards them.

Now there were hundreds of dogs. They were coming from everywhere. They were climbing over garden gates, squeezing through hedges, and jumping out of kitchen windows.

"Jesslebink!" screamed
Matthew, as the first dog
reached him and started to
lick.

"Fafflepit," said Tom, as a
huge dog put its paws on his
shoulders.

The boys were soon on the
ground, and every dog that
could reach them was licking
like mad. There was a

mountain of slobbering dogs on top of them and a forest of wagging tails.

"Urrrrrrrrr!"

"Ahhhhhhhhhh!"

"Woof, slobber, slobber, woof!"

At last the owners arrived.

"Fido!"

"Lassie!"

"Benjie!"

"Popsy!"

"Hector!"

"Pepper!"

"Come here at once!"

"Leave those boys alone!"

The dogs were dragged away and the boys were helped

to their feet. Their lunch-boxes
had burst open on the ground,
and a scruffy old mongrel was
gobbling up the last sandwich.

"Batscum!" yelled Tom,
hitting out at the dog.

The old mongrel dodged the
blow, and then cocked its leg
over one of the lunch-boxes
and trotted away.

Chapter Five

Tom and Matthew arrived
late for school. Their clothes
were torn and they were
covered in slobbery licks.

But Mr Bentwhistle said nothing.

This morning he was wearing a green cloak and a pair of black boots. A bright orange shirt was tucked into his jeans.

He paced up and down the classroom, humming, while Class 4 settled down to their work. Once or twice he sniffed the air and muttered "Higglefizz" to himself.

At lunch-time, he walked over to Tom and Matthew.

"*Hungry*, boys?" he asked, winking at them.

Tom and Matthew said nothing. They were thinking of their empty lunch-boxes.

Mr Bentwhistle strode off towards the dining-hall.

"Grattlefunk?" suggested Matthew.

Tom nodded and they ran after Mr Bentwhistle. They rushed up to the dinner lady who was serving out the food.

"Grattlefunk," said Tom.

"Addlespook," said Matthew.

After a puzzled glance, the
dinner lady shrugged her
shoulders and ignored them.
She went on filling her ladle
with dollops of mince and
thumping it on to plates.

The smell of mince and gravy and vegetables reached Tom and Matthew. They both sniffed. The dinner lady looked up at them.

"Yes, boys?"

"Biddlepoof," said Tom and Matthew together.

The dinner lady frowned. "That's enough of your cheek, lads. You are holding up the others. Take your lunch-boxes and go and sit down."

"Puddlefunk," said Tom.

"Gruntlers!" shouted Matthew.

The dinner lady started to go rather red in the face. "That's enough," she repeated.

"Huddlesmash!" yelled Tom.

The dinner lady went even redder. She looked round the room and spotted the caretaker.

"Mr Jones," she called.

Mr Jones came over. He was a big, strong man.

"What's the trouble?" he asked.

"It's these two. They're giving me a lot of cheek."

Mr Jones folded his arms and grinned at the boys.

"What's the matter, lads? Have you forgotten your lunch-boxes?"

"Bootlefug," said Matthew.

"Addlespook," said Tom.

"See what I mean?" said the dinner lady. The next dollop of mince landed with a splat on the plate and sprayed three children with gravy.

Matthew tried to explain. "Huddlesmash. Diddle bing gruntlers."

Tom nodded. "Puddlefunk," he said.

"Enough!" yelled Mr Jones. He grabbed Tom and Matthew and pushed them in front of him.

"I'm taking you to the headteacher," he said grimly, as they reached the door.

Tom looked at Matthew. "Grumperoonie!" he shouted.

They both wriggled free from Mr Jones and sprinted outside. In the playground, they almost crashed into Mr Bentwhistle.

"Here, boys," he said calmly, as they skidded round him. "You'll need some money for food."

He threw them a little red bag, and then turned on his heel and went back inside.

"Mind the cat," he said, just before he disappeared.

Chapter Six

The school cat lay in a patch
of sunlight, cleaning herself.
  Suddenly she sat up and
sniffed.

Then she gave a loud yowl and chased after the boys as they ran off towards the supermarket.

In no time, she was joined by more cats. Thin cats, fat cats, ginger cats, tabby cats, black cats, young cats, old cats.

Pouncing round corners,
leaping down from walls, all on
the scent of Higglefizz.

Matthew turned round.
"Crunchibat!" he yelled.

Tom looked too. "Swiddle!"
he said.

They ran faster and faster,
but the cats were catching up.
At last the boys reached the
supermarket and pushed the
doors open.

Outside, a crowd of cats
pressed furry faces to the glass
and yowled.

Inside, Tom and Matthew
grabbed a few things from the
shelves and then lined up at the

checkout. Matthew emptied Mr
Bentwhistle's red bag on to the
counter. He didn't look at the
coins. He was too busy eating
crisps.

"What's your game, young man?" said the checkout lady. She didn't sound too friendly.

Matthew looked at the counter. It was covered in toy money!

"Grumperoonie!" shouted Tom.

They crashed out of the supermarket.

"Stop those boys!" screamed the checkout lady.

Chapter Seven

Tom and Matthew ran up the hill which led out of the town. Behind them came hundreds of cats. Behind the cats were the dinner lady, Mr Jones, the checkout lady and a policeman.

"Stop!" shouted the policeman, blowing his whistle.

"Stop!" squeaked the dinner lady.

"Stop!" screamed the checkout lady.

"Stop!" yelled Mr Jones.

Tom and Matthew ran on.

The policeman got into his car and the dinner lady, Mr Jones and the checkout lady all squeezed in the back.

The police car roared up the hill through the crowd of cats. They leapt out of the way and landed in spitting heaps on each side of the road.

Matthew and Tom kept

running, in search of a hiding-place. Somewhere they could stay until the fuss had died down.

Just ahead they saw a stile, which led into a field. Tom and Matthew climbed over it and started to run across the field.

The police car screeched to a halt and the policeman, the checkout lady, Mr Jones and the dinner lady all tumbled out. They scrambled over the stile and ran after the boys.

There were a lot of sheep in the field. At first they took no notice of the two boys or the four grown-ups. Then one sheep lifted its head and sniffed. Then another did the same, and another, and another.

It was as if the first sheep had said to the others, "I smell Higglefizz!" for soon the whole flock of sheep was running towards the boys.

"Hey, what the –" said Mr Jones, as five sheep shot past him, tripping him up and sending him flying on to the grass.

"Help!" shrieked the checkout lady.

The red-faced dinner lady stood by the fence, swinging her ladle. She swiped at the woolly bottoms as they sped past.

"Take that!" she yelled.

Only the policeman was ahead of the sheep. He was young and fit and he was catching up with the boys.

So were the sheep!

Matthew was tired. He felt
he couldn't run another step.
The policeman was getting
nearer and nearer, until at last
he was right beside Matthew.

"Come on, lad," he said, quite kindly. "You and your friend are causing a lot of trouble."

"Higglefizz," panted Matthew.

The policeman looked puzzled. He was just about to answer, when the first sheep arrived.

Thump! The sheep knocked into them and started to lick Matthew.

Thump! Thump! Thump! More sheep arrived. They were coming thick and fast. Soon Matthew and the policeman were completely hidden by them.

A little way ahead, Tom was in trouble too. He was trapped by sheep, all trying to lick him. He began to shout, "Rippleskim!"

The policeman was shouting too. "Get away, you silly animals!"

But the sheep took no notice.

They crowded round Tom and they crowded round Matthew and the policeman.

"Help, they're crushing us!" yelled the policeman.

The other grown-ups stood in a group, staring at the boys and the sheep and the policeman.

"Go and get the –" began the policeman, but at that moment he was knocked down to the ground by an eager sheep.

While he was being pushed and licked, Tom looked round for a way of escape, but there was none. He started to panic.

They were going to be trampled to death. Just because they'd taken the Higglefizz from Mr Bentwhistle's house.

"I'm sorry!" he shouted.

To his surprise, the words came out right.

He tried again. "Mr Bentwhistle. I'm sorry. We're both sorry!"

When Matthew heard Tom's voice, he looked up. And then he saw something he hadn't noticed before.

In the next field was a tall yellow house! Mr Bentwhistle's house. And coming out of the door was Mr Bentwhistle, with a box under his arm.

"Mr Bentwhistle!" yelled Matthew.

Mr Bentwhistle started to run. He seemed to float over the ground with his huge strides. In no time, he was at the edge of the field. He climbed over the gate and came running towards them.

He was opening a box as he
ran.

It was a box they'd seen
before. A pink box.

Mr Bentwhistle was grinning and his eyebrows were shooting up and down.

"Wetlip!" he shouted, waving the box at them.

"Wetlip!" he said again, as he turned the box upside down and started to shake it.

A small scrap of paper fell out.

Then the strangest thing happened. Suddenly there were brightly coloured clouds all over the field. They floated over the sheep and the boys and the policeman. Then they

floated over the checkout lady,
Mr Jones and the dinner lady.

"Wetlip!" shouted Mr
Bentwhistle again, rubbing his
hands together.

"Wetlip!" he repeated, as his
eyes followed the floating
clouds.

"Wetlip! The best thing a
teacher can have. The best
thing *anyone* can have. There's
no muddle too muddly for
Wetlip. No pickle too pickly.
No higgle too fizzy."

The grown-ups watched. The
boys watched. The sheep
watched. Everything was
suddenly very still as the

coloured clouds floated above the field.

"Wetlip," whispered Matthew.

"Wetlip," said the policeman, as he got up from his knees and straightened up his uniform.

"Wetlip," echoed the checkout lady, Mr Jones and the dinner lady.

Then, very slowly, everything started to fade away. First the clouds, then the sheep, then the field, then the grown-ups, and, last of all, Tom, Mr Bentwhistle and the box of Wetlip.

Matthew was alone. For a
moment, he could see nothing
but a sort of mist.

Then the mist began to clear and he looked around him.

He was back in the classroom.

Matthew rubbed his eyes. Everything seemed normal. He looked at his watch to check the time. He stared at it. It *couldn't* be right! He shook it, held it to his ear, then looked again.

It was a digital watch and it told the time and the date.

He simply couldn't believe it!

It said Monday the fifth of September. The first day of term!

Chapter Eight

Tom burst into the classroom.
"I've seen him! The new
teacher. I've seen him!"

The rest of the class crowded
round Tom.

"What's he like?"

"I dunno. Sort of ordinary."

"How old is he?"

Tom shrugged. "Quite old. At least thirty."

"What's he look like?"

"Oh, just like most teachers." Then he added, "He looks friendly though. He smiled at me."

It was as though Mr Bentwhistle had never been real. The rest of the class didn't seem to remember anything about him. Only Tom and Matthew remembered.

Tom came over to Matthew and whispered, "There's

something about him. I think
I've seen him somewhere
before."

"Is it Mr Bentwhistle?"
asked Matthew.

Tom shook his head. "I don't
know. He looks a bit like him.
But –"

Just then, the door opened and the new teacher came in.

He was extremely tall and thin, with a big beaky nose, frizzy hair and dark bushy eyebrows. He moved his eyebrows up and down very fast, sometimes together and sometimes not.

But Tom was right. He was quite ordinary. He said the same things as other teachers and he did the same things.

The first half of the first morning of the first day of term went quickly.

"I like him," whispered Tom, as the bell went for break.

Matthew nodded. "Yeah, he's OK."

The new teacher picked up his books and headed for the door. Then he stopped, turned round and looked straight at Tom and Matthew.

He smiled. And then he winked.

"It *is* him, after all!" said Tom, as he followed the others out of the classroom.

Matthew said nothing. He walked up to the table at the

front of the class. The teacher's table. He stood there and waited until everyone else had gone out. Everyone except Tom.

"Come on," said Tom, "let's go."

Still Matthew said nothing. He opened the drawer in the teacher's table and searched inside it.

"What are you doing?" said Tom. "What are you looking for?"

Matthew didn't answer. He searched some more, then suddenly he grinned.

"I *thought* so," he said at

last, and took something out
from the drawer.

In the palm of his hand lay a
tiny pink box.

Tom gasped. Although it was much smaller, it was exactly like the box that Mr Bentwhistle had been carrying when he saved them from the sheep and the grown-ups and the Higglefizz.

"Wetlip," whispered Tom.

Being careful not to disturb it, Matthew replaced the box and shut the drawer.

He let out a long sigh.

"That's all right then," he said.